THOMAS & FRIENDS™

TRAVELING TALES

Random House New York

Contents

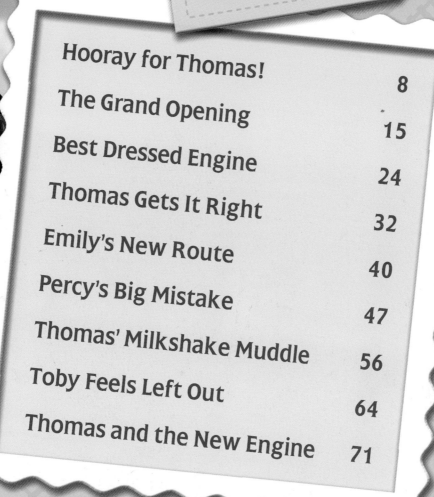

Thomas the Tank Engine & Friends™

CREATED BY BRITT ALLCROFT

Based on The Railway Series by The Reverend W Awdry.
© 2005, 2006, 2007, 2010 Gullane (Thomas) LLC.
Thomas the Tank Engine & Friends and Thomas & Friends are trademarks of Gullane (Thomas) Limited.
HIT and the HIT Entertainment logo are trademarks of HIT Entertainment Limited.
All rights reserved. Published in the United States by Random House Children's Books, a division of
Random House, Inc., 1745 Broadway, New York, NY 10019, and in Canada by Random House of Canada
Limited, Toronto. Originally published by Random House, Inc., as *Hooray for Thomas!* in 2005, *Track
Stars!* in 2006, and *Thomas' Milkshake Muddle* in 2007.
Random House and the colophon are registered trademarks of Random House, Inc.

HiT entertainment

www.randomhouse.com/kids
www.thomasandfriends.com

Library of Congress Control Number: 2009941701
ISBN 978-0-375-86087-4
MANUFACTURED IN SINGAPORE
10 9 8 7 6 5 4 3 2 1

• Hooray for Thomas! •

It was an exciting day on the Island of Sodor.

"Good morning," called Harold.

Annie and Clarabel were full of happy children. Thomas was taking them to their annual Sports Day. Everything was ready for the day to begin.

"I do hope I'm Number One and win a medal," said a boy.

"It must be splendid to win a medal," chuffed Thomas. "After all, I'm Engine Number One!"

Thomas worked hard all afternoon. But he couldn't stop thinking about medals. He imagined himself wearing a gold medal on a bright red ribbon. How smart he would look!

"Hello, Thomas," whistled Percy. "I'm taking Sir Topham Hatt to Sports Day."

"You can see the egg-and-spoon race," chuffed Thomas.

"I didn't know eggs and spoons had races."

"The *children* race with eggs on spoons," said Bertie.

"And the winner gets a medal— I wish *I* could have a medal."

"You need to win a race first!" whistled Percy.

"*I'll* race you, Thomas. The first one to the station is the winner!"

"You're on," called Thomas.

"Ready,
          steady,
                  GO!"

"Better hurry, Bertie!"
peeped Thomas.

Then Thomas had to
stop to pick up some
passengers.

"Better hurry, Thomas!"
teased Bertie as he rattled over
the bridge.

Then Bertie had to stop at a level
crossing.

"Last one there puffs hot air!"
called Thomas.

Thomas was nearly at the station.

As he drew near the playing field, a signalman flagged him down. Now Thomas was really cross. Bertie was sure to win.

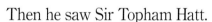

Then he saw Sir Topham Hatt.

"Thomas, the Sports Day medals have been left in my office. You must fetch them at once. We can't let the children down."

"Of course not, Sir," replied Thomas. And he chuffed away.

Meanwhile, Bertie had raced into the station.

"I won!" shouted Bertie. "I won!" And he waited eagerly for Thomas. He waited and waited.

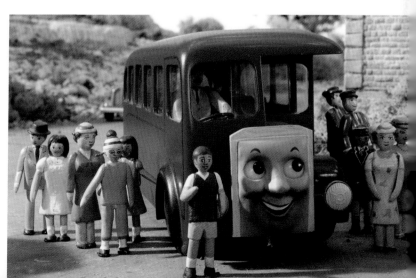

But Thomas had forgotten about the race. He was thinking about the children.

"I can't let them down . . . I can't let them down."

At last, Thomas puffed back into the big station. The Station Master gave Thomas' Driver the box of medals.

Then Thomas set off again. He arrived *just* in time!

"Well done," said Sir Topham Hatt.
"Thank you, Sir," panted Thomas.
Sir Topham Hatt presented the medals to the winners.
"Congratulations!"
"Thank you, Sir!"

The next day, Bertie and the medal winner arrived with a surprise for Thomas.

A small boy presented *him* with a gold medal on a red ribbon.

"You were very helpful at Sports Day."

"So we thought you should have a medal of your own," added the boy.

"My very own medal!" said Thomas. "Thank you."

"Three cheers for Thomas, the Number One Engine! Hip, hip, hooray!"

"But I still won the race," tooted Bertie.

· The Grand Opening ·

The engines on the mountain railway were excited.
They were helping to build a new line.

It would take visitors to even more beautiful places
on the Island of Sodor.

Sir Topham Hatt arrived with important news.

"The Grand Opening is this afternoon. I want to see the new line from the air. Lady Hatt and I will arrive on Harold the Helicopter."

Just then, Skarloey chugged in.

"You're late for the announcement," complained Sir Topham Hatt. "Really Useful Engines are never late."

"I'm sorry, Sir."

At the airfield, there was another problem.

"Engine trouble," said the Pilot. "Harold's not going anywhere today."

Lady Hatt was most upset. "But I've been looking forward to the Grand Opening all week."

"And I, my dear, will find a solution."

And he did.
"Topham, you cannot be serious. Me, ride in this?"
"The wind direction is perfect. We'll be there in no time."

Soon the hot-air balloon rose into the sky.

But Skarloey was upset. "All this extra work is going to make me late again!"

The hot-air balloon was floating peacefully through the sky.

Lady Hatt was enjoying herself. "The new line looks splendid!" she said.

"Thank you, my dear," replied Sir Topham Hatt.

Down the track, the workmen were still loading their ladders.
"Hurry up, hurry up," Skarloey puffed.

"If Skarloey doesn't hurry," sighed Sir Topham Hatt, "he'll be late again!"

All the engines were ready for the Grand Opening.

"Where's Skarloey?" Rusty asked.

"He promised to be on time," said Peter Sam.

At last, Skarloey was on his way.

Then there was trouble. The balloon's flames suddenly went out. The air in the balloon cooled and the balloon started to fall.

"Hold tight," the Pilot called.

"I want to get out," demanded Lady Hatt.

"Not now, dear," said Sir Topham Hatt.

"The balloon's going to land in the tree," cried Skarloey.

And it came down right in front of Skarloey.

"There's Sir Topham Hatt."

"My hat is ruined," cried Lady Hatt.

"So is mine," said Sir Topham Hatt.

"Don't worry!" called Skarloey's Driver. "We'll soon have you down."

"Am I glad to see *you*, Skarloey."

"Thank you, Sir."

Before long, Sir Topham Hatt and Lady Hatt were safely on the ground. They boarded Skarloey's boxcar and set off at once.

Everyone was waiting as Skarloey brought his important passengers to the Grand Opening.

Sir Topham Hatt declared the new line open.

"With special thanks to Skarloey," he said, "for helping us get here!"

Everyone cheered.

"Even so, you were *still* late!" teased Rusty.

"I know," said Skarloey. "But because I was late, Sir Topham Hatt was right on time!"

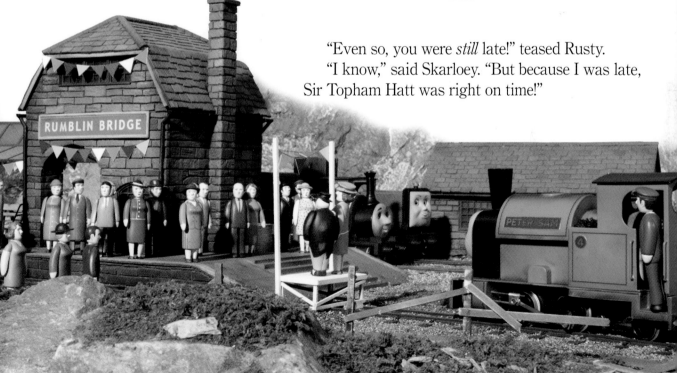

• Best Dressed Engine •

It was May Day on the Island of Sodor and the engines were celebrating. They knew there'd be music and lots of fun.

The station was being decorated. Sir Topham Hatt said that the engines could be decorated, too.

"I'm going to have flags and streamers!" whistled Percy.

"I'm going to have a big red banner," whistled Thomas.

"What decorations will you have, Gordon?" asked Murdoch.

"Decorations aren't dignified for an important engine like me. I pull the Express!" Gordon was feeling insulted. "Humpf! Silly little engines," he grunted.

Thomas was enjoying himself. He was bringing the maypole.
The farmer's children waved. Thomas peeped happily as he
passed by.

Soon it was time for the
decorating.
Percy's Driver was
wrapping streamers and
flags around his funnel.
Thomas had a big red
banner on his tanks.

Even Murdoch was being decorated. Although he was very shy about it.

"We could have a contest for the Best Dressed Engine," suggested James.

Just then, Gordon shunted in. "A contest!" he puffed. "I'm bound to win any contest."

"You will have to be decorated," said James. "This is a Best Dressed Engine contest."

"Not me!" puffed Gordon. "You'd never catch *me* looking so ridiculous!"

The engines felt splendid.

But not Gordon . . . he was cross. "Decorations aren't dignified. Ha! Who cares about a contest anyway?"

Further down his line, a colorful banner was strung across the bridge.

Then, as Gordon steamed across the bridge, it came loose and wrapped around his firebox. Gordon couldn't see the line ahead!

Gordon tried to *whoosh* the banner off, but it wouldn't budge.

"I can't see!" he whistled loudly to his Driver. "Stop!"

"You *can't* stop, Gordon," his Driver called back. "You're the Express!"

Trevor was chugging slowly along with his load of apples for the children's apple bob.

Trevor heard a whistle. He was going as fast as he could.

But it wasn't fast enough.

The apples were all smashed!

James was the last engine to join the contest—or so he thought!
"Here comes Gordon," cried the passengers.

"We didn't think you wanted to be decorated," teased Thomas.

"I didn't," huffed Gordon.

"Well, you're definitely the Best Dressed Engine," said James.

All the engines agreed.

Gordon was secretly pleased. But he didn't think it was dignified to say so. Silly Gordon!

• Thomas Gets It Right •

It had been a stormy night on the Island of Sodor. Telegraph poles had blown down. Tiles had blown off the station roofs. And branches had fallen onto the lines. All over the Island, the storm had made a terrible mess.

Sir Topham Hatt came to Tidmouth Sheds.

"The storm has caused confusion and delay," he boomed. "So you must all be Really Useful Engines."

"I'll be the *most* useful engine," boasted James.

"No, I will," sniffed Gordon. "I'm the fastest—*I'll* do the most journeys."

Thomas hoped he could finish his Special Delivery as quickly as possible. He wanted to do the most journeys and be the most useful engine of all.

Soon all the engines were steaming away from Tidmouth Sheds.

James went to Knapford Yard to pick up the workmen.

Gordon went to the goods yard to collect telegraph poles.

Toby trundled to collect new roof tiles.

33

And Thomas steamed over to Maron Station. Farmer
McColl was waiting for Thomas. Next to him were boxes
and boxes of newly laid eggs.

"These fresh eggs are needed across the Island," said
Farmer McColl.

The station staff quickly loaded Thomas' freight cars with
the eggs, and Thomas was raring to go.

"My eggs must be delivered safely," said Farmer McColl. "So I am coming to
make sure you go slowly and carefully."

"Slowly," *wheesh*ed Thomas sadly. He wanted to finish his job quickly and
make lots of journeys. Thomas gave one sad *toot* of his whistle and slowly
pulled away.

Thomas trundled on. He huffed and puffed as gently as he could.

Thomas had to stop at a crossing.

Gordon steamed by. "Fastest and best," he chirruped.

Gordon looked very happy. Thomas felt very sad.

Thomas pulled into Maithwaite Station.

James was waiting. He was carrying workmen. They were fixing the station-house roof. Station staff unloaded four boxes of eggs for the village store.

"How many journeys have you done?" asked James brightly.

"This is my first," said Thomas.

"Ha!" huffed James. "I'm on my third. I'm as red as a rocket and twice as fast!" And he steamed quickly out of the station.

Thomas was upset. He wanted to go fast more than ever.

Now the eggs were unloaded, and Thomas chuffed slowly out of the station.

35

Thomas puffed across the countryside—very, very slowly.

Then Thomas saw Toby taking on coal in a siding. His freight cars were full of roof tiles. Toby was having a wonderful day.

"I'm on my second journey," he whistled proudly.

Thomas was very sad. Toby rushed past him. It made Thomas want to go faster than ever! "Even Toby has made more journeys than me," he moaned. "It's not fair—I can be fast *and* careful."

So Thomas started to speed up!

"Fast *and* careful, fast *and* careful," he huffed happily.

But Thomas was going so fast, he *wasn't* being careful.

Farmer McColl was worried. "Slow down, Thomas," he called. "You will break my eggs."

But Thomas was going so quickly, he didn't hear Farmer McColl. And he didn't slow down. He went even faster! The eggs started to bounce in their boxes.

Then Thomas changed lines. It caused a big bump! The eggs were breaking!!

Thomas came to a junction. He had to slow down.

"Stop, Thomas!" cried Farmer McColl. "You have broken my eggs!"

This time Thomas did hear Farmer McColl, and he stopped right away.

"Cinders and ashes!" he cried.

But Farmer McColl was still cross.

Thomas felt bad. "I'm sorry," he whistled. "I just wanted to be Really Useful."

Farmer McColl checked his eggs. Luckily, only a few were broken.

Now Thomas knew he had to go slowly. So he pulled away as gently as he could.

Thomas headed for Brendam Docks. Suddenly he heard an impatient *toot*.

James was behind him. He blew his whistle loudly.

But Thomas knew he couldn't speed up. "Sometimes going slowly can be just as important as going fast," said Thomas. And he puffed carefully on.

That evening, Sir Topham Hatt came to Tidmouth Sheds. He looked very pleased. "You have all worked hard and been Really Useful Engines," he said proudly.

The engines were very happy. Except for Thomas. He was thinking about the broken eggs.

"I only made one journey, Sir," he said. "And I broke Farmer McColl's eggs."

"But most of the eggs were delivered safely," boomed Sir Topham Hatt. "Farmer McColl gave the broken ones to me. And I love having scrambled eggs for my breakfast. You, Thomas," he added, "are a Really Useful Engine."

Thomas just beamed.

• Emily's New Route •

It was summertime on the Island of Sodor. All the engines were very busy. They carried freight and passengers up and down the lines.

Sir Topham Hatt came to see Emily. "I am opening some new routes for the summer," he announced. "Emily, you will pull the Flour Mill Special."

"Thank you, Sir," said Emily. She was pleased.

Emily stopped to fill up with water on the way to the flour mill. But James was already there.

40

"Sir Topham Hatt has given me the Flour Mill Special," said Emily.

"You're lucky," James huffed. "I have to do the Black Loch Run."

"Why don't you like going to Black Loch?" asked Emily.

"There are boulders all over the tracks," he moaned. "They bash your buffers and scratch your paint. And there's the Black Loch Monster!"

"What's the Black Loch Monster?"

"Nobody knows," said James. "Black figures move in the water and then they disappear."

"Ooohhhhh!"

And James puffed away.

Emily was pleased *she* didn't have to go to Black Loch.

At the flour mill, the flour had been loaded onto trucks. Emily was coupled up. Then she puffed across the countryside to Knapford Station.

But the Troublesome Trucks saw a chance for mischief. "Hold back, hold back," they screeched.

Emily pulled as hard as she could, but the Troublesome Trucks made her go very slowly.

Emily was late delivering the flour, so there would be no fresh bread that day.

Sir Topham Hatt was cross. "This means I won't have any toast or muffins for breakfast. If you are late again, you will have to do the Black Loch Run instead of James."

Emily didn't want to have her buffers bashed by boulders. And she didn't want to see the Black Loch Monster. "I must get the flour to the station on time," Emily puffed.

The next morning, the Troublesome Trucks tricked her again. "Off we go, off we go!" they chuckled. But they weren't coupled up properly. "Mustn't be late, mustn't be late," they giggled. So Emily puffed quickly away.

But only half the Troublesome Trucks went with her.

Emily arrived at the station.

"But you've only brought *half* the flour!" the Station Master cried.

So Emily had to go back for the rest of the Troublesome Trucks. "Oh, no!" Emily cried. "I don't want to get the Black Loch Run."

When Emily arrived at the mill, the trucks were more troublesome than ever. "Emily the late engine, Emily the late engine," they sang.

This made Emily *very* cross, and she biffed them, very hard.

"Oh, no!" they cried. And they splashed into the duck pond.

Emily was covered in a floury mess.

That evening Sir Topham Hatt came to see Emily. "Emily, you have caused confusion and delay," Sir Topham Hatt said. "Now you are to take over the Black Loch Run."

Emily was very unhappy.

"Wait until you've tried it," Thomas puffed. "The Black Loch Run might be nice."

"I don't think so," Emily moaned. "Bashed buffers and a big monster. It sounds miserable to me."

The next morning, Emily puffed sadly to the station. Lots of excited children and vacationers climbed on board.

"They're all looking forward to their vacation," she thought. "I mustn't let them down."

Soon Emily was steaming up hills and through valleys. "I bet it won't last," she said to herself.

Emily reached the murky waters of Black Loch. "Ohhh . . . that's where the monster's supposed to be," she puffed nervously.

Then there was trouble. Rocks fell and blocked the line.

"Oh, no!" Emily had to wait for help. "I knew I wouldn't like this route!" she huffed.

Suddenly she saw something dark and mysterious moving in the water. "And now the monster's coming," Emily gasped.

Emily was scared. Her boiler quivered and her valves rattled. She wanted to steam away. "I never want to see Black Loch again!" she cried.

But Emily thought of the children in the coach behind her. She was determined to get them to their vacation, whatever it took.

At last the water settled, and Emily saw what the monster really was.

"It's a family of seals." Emily was delighted.

The children were delighted, too.

Soon the line was cleared. Emily steamed on through the countryside. The children would reach their vacation on time.

That evening, Thomas and Emily both stopped to watch the seals.

"You were right," said Emily. "Black Loch *is* a nice route after all."

• Percy's Big Mistake •

Percy is a little green engine who can shunt and pull. He pulls both passengers and freight. At the Docks—and at the Quarry. Percy's favorite job is carrying the mail. But sometimes Percy has so much to do, he ends up running late.

One evening Percy arrived late at Brendam Docks.

"You're late again, Percy," said the Dock Manager. "I will have to speak to Sir Topham Hatt."

Percy was upset.

Percy returned to Tidmouth Sheds. The other engines were already asleep. Then Percy heard voices on the other side of the Sheds. It was Sir Topham Hatt! And he was talking to Percy's Driver. Percy tried not to listen, but he couldn't help himself!

"Percy has been late too often this week," said Sir Topham Hatt. "He must go to the scrap yards tomorrow."

"Sir Topham Hatt wants to scrap me!" gasped Percy. Percy worried all night long.

The next morning, the sun shone and the birds sang, but Percy was too upset to notice.

"Sir Topham Hatt wants to scrap me!" he cried. "And all because I was late."

"Sir Topham Hatt wouldn't scrap a Really Useful Engine," said Thomas. "And you, Percy, are a Really Useful Engine."

Percy felt better, until he noticed the time.

"I'm going to be late!" he cried.

Percy *wheesh*ed away. If he was on time, maybe Sir Topham Hatt wouldn't send him to the scrap yards.

Percy's first job was collecting pipes from Brendam Docks. But when he arrived, Cranky was still unloading.

"Hurry up, slowcoach," *wheesh*ed Percy. "I *must* be on time!"

"I'll take as long as I like," said Cranky. And he went slower than ever.

The moment Cranky had finished, Percy took off. He hadn't waited for the pipes to be tied down. Percy rounded the bend. The pipes slipped and fell all over the track, but Percy puffed on.

Percy thought he had delivered the pipes, so he chuffed away to his next job.

Percy was to take some tar wagons to the workmen mending the roads.

"Be careful," said his Driver. "Tar is sticky stuff."

But Percy wasn't being careful. He was going too fast. Percy charged down Gordon's Hill. He didn't see Gordon and the Express until it was too late. The brake van passed Gordon—but the tar wagons didn't!

Luckily, no one was hurt, but Gordon was very cross.

"Now look what you've done!" he *wheesh*ed. "What will Sir Topham Hatt say?"

Percy thought he knew. "Oh, no!" he cried. "I'm *sure* to be scrapped now!" And so Percy decided to run away. . . .

Harvey was clearing away the tar wagons when Sir Topham Hatt arrived aboard Thomas. "Where is Percy?" he said. "He has caused confusion and delay!" Gordon didn't know. "He just left very quickly, Sir."

"He heard you at the Sheds, Sir," said Thomas. "He thought you were sending him to be scrapped."

"Hmmm, I think I need a word with Percy," said Sir Topham Hatt. "You must all help me find him."

And so everyone looked for Percy. They searched high—and they searched low. They looked to and fro, but they couldn't see Percy anywhere.

"What's to become of me?" Percy whispered, but there was no one around to hear. Percy looked very small and felt very lonely.

Thomas and Sir Topham Hatt were looking for Percy on Thomas' Branch Line.

Thomas suddenly had an idea. "I think I know where Percy is, Sir." And he puffed back to Tidmouth Sheds as fast as he could.

The Sheds were very quiet as Thomas rolled into the engine berths.

"Percy?" called Sir Topham Hatt. "Are you there?"

"Please don't scrap me, Sir," he said. "I didn't mean to be late or cause trouble."

"Scrap you?" boomed Sir Topham Hatt. "Why, the very thought of it!"

And Sir Topham Hatt told Percy what he had *really* said. "I told your Driver you had been working too hard, and *that* was why you were late. I had decided that after taking some scrap to the smelters, you were to carry the mail—all week!"

Percy was as happy as he had ever been. "Do you really mean it, Sir?" puffed Percy proudly. "The mail—for a whole week! Thank you, Sir!" Percy couldn't stop himself tooting for joy.

Thomas tooted, too. It was good to have his friend back.

So Percy carried the mail all week. He wasn't late and he didn't make a mistake—not one!

And Percy decided never to listen to silly stories ever again.

Especially not ones made up by himself!

•Thomas' Milkshake Muddle•

Once a year, the children of Sodor are all invited to a special summer party. There was to be ice cream and cake for everyone.

Every engine wanted to be the one to take the children to the party. On the day of the party, Sir Topham Hatt came to Tidmouth Sheds.

Thomas hoped that *he* would be taking the children, but Sir Topham Hatt chose Emily.

He had other jobs for Thomas.

"Thomas, first you are to go to the Dairy to collect milk to make the ice cream. Then you must go to the farm on the other side of the Island to collect butter for cakes. All in time for the children's party."

Thomas set off proudly.

When Thomas arrived at the Dairy, the Manager told him he was to take the milk churns to the Ice Cream Factory. "You have to go *very* slowly," he told Thomas.

So Thomas steamed carefully away.

When Thomas stopped at a signal, he met Emily.

"Hello, slowcoach!" she whistled.

"I'm not being a slowcoach!" huffed Thomas. "I'm being reliable!"

"If you weren't a slowcoach," Emily sniffed, "Sir Topham Hatt would have given you my job! I'm fast and I'm reliable. That's why I'm taking the children!"

Emily looked very pleased with herself.

This made Thomas cross. "I can be as fast as you!" he huffed.

"I'll race you to the next signal!" Emily whistled. And she steamed quickly away.

Thomas *wheesh*ed after her as fast as his pistons would pump! As he raced along, the milk churns rattled and rocked. . . .

They biffed and bashed. . . .

And at the next signal, Thomas raced ahead of Emily.

Thomas was very pleased.

He steamed off for the Ice Cream Factory, but he had completely forgotten about going slowly.

The Ice Cream Factory Manager was very happy. Thomas had delivered the milk in record time! Now the factory could make the ice cream for the party.

But when the Manager looked into one of the churns, he was very surprised.

"This milk is almost butter!" exclaimed the Manager.

The Factory Manager asked Thomas if the churns had rattled around. Thomas looked worried. "If you shake milk for long enough, it turns to butter," he told Thomas.

Thomas was very upset.

The Factory Manager was cross. "You must go back to the Dairy and get more milk. And remember to go *slowly* this time!" he said sternly.

Thomas steamed back to the Dairy as fast as he could. When Thomas arrived back at the Dairy, Sir Topham Hatt was there. He was very cross! "Thomas, it is nearly time for the party, and you still have not collected the butter from the other side of the Island. The children will have no cakes for the party."

Thomas felt terrible.

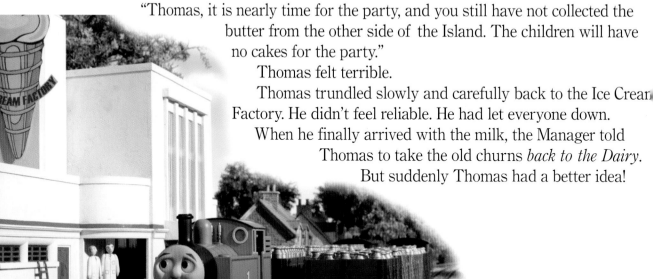

Thomas trundled slowly and carefully back to the Ice Cream Factory. He didn't feel reliable. He had let everyone down.

When he finally arrived with the milk, the Manager told Thomas to take the old churns *back to the Dairy*.

But suddenly Thomas had a better idea!

Thomas steamed along with the milk churns even faster than he had before. He huffed up Gordon's Hill . . . and chuffed down to the Valley. He raced like a rocket . . . and he *wheesh*ed like the wind.

The churns in Thomas' freight cars rattled and rolled . . . they clanked and crashed . . . and biffed and bashed. Even the cows and sheep looked up to see what the noise was. But Thomas couldn't stop until he got to the bakery!

As he arrived, he blew his whistle long and hard.
Peeppeeeeeeeeeeeep!

"I need butter, not milk!" cried the Baker. He was
surprised to see the milk churns.

"Look inside the churns!" tooted Thomas.

The Baker couldn't believe his eyes! The "almost-butter" was now butter! Enough to make *all* the cakes for the party!

Sir Topham Hatt had heard what Thomas had done. He came to see him. Thomas thought Sir Topham Hatt would be cross. He was very worried.

But Sir Topham Hatt smiled. "Thomas, you have saved the children's party!" he boomed. "So today, that makes you the most reliable engine on the whole of Sodor!"

And later, Thomas had his most important job yet—as Guest of Honor at the children's party! There was lots of ice cream and plenty of cakes. Everyone had a wonderful time. The children cheered for Thomas.

Thomas felt very proud.

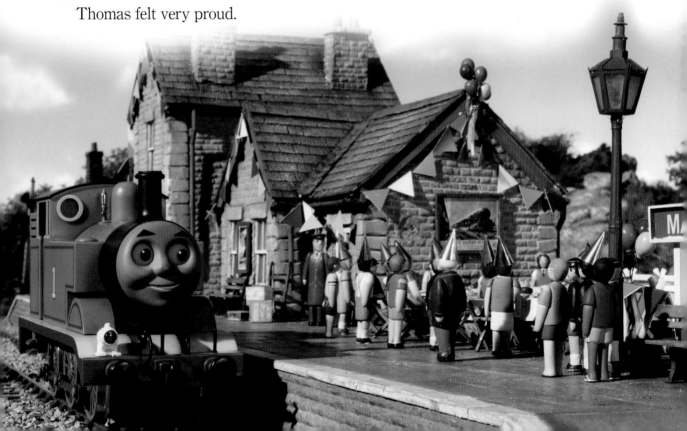

•Toby Feels Left Out•

It was springtime on the Island of Sodor. All the engines were working hard in the sunshine.

One morning, Sir Topham Hatt arrived at Tidmouth Sheds. He had some exciting news. "The new Sodor Museum opens soon," he announced. "Lots of very important people will be coming to the Island for the Grand Opening."

"What's a museum?" asked Percy.

"It's a place where they put *old* things so people can stand and look at them," huffed Gordon.

"I want you all to look your best, so everyone is to have a repaint."

All the engines were very pleased.

Later that morning, Toby met James at Knapford Station. "Have you heard about the opening of the new museum?" puffed James. "We're all having a repaint. I shall look wonderful with a brand-new coat of red paint."

"I've not heard about that," said Toby. "Why hasn't Sir Topham Hatt told me?"

"You must have been left out," chuffed James, and he steamed away.

That night, Toby couldn't sleep. He kept worrying about what James had said. "Why hasn't Sir Topham Hatt told me about the museum?" he wondered. "Why have I been left out?"

By the next morning, Toby thought he knew the answer. He met Thomas at Abbey Station.

"Have *you* heard about the museum?" asked Toby.

"Yes," puffed Thomas excitedly. "We're all being repainted!"

"I'm not," puffed Toby sadly. "But I think I know why. I am a very old steam tram. Maybe Sir Topham Hatt has decided to put me inside the museum."

Thomas wasn't so sure. "Why don't you ask him?" huffed Thomas helpfully.

Toby looked worried. He was frightened of what Sir Topham Hatt might say.

"Must go," puffed Thomas. "Really Useful Engines are really busy ones." And he chuffed away.

Toby thought for a moment. "I'll show Sir Topham Hatt that he can't put me in a museum," said Toby. "I'll show him *I'm* a Really Useful Engine."

Toby arrived at Tidmouth Sheds. Sir Topham Hatt was talking to Emily.
"Emily, you must go to the Yard for your repaint," said Sir Topham Hatt.
Emily was very happy.

"Another engine must collect your flour," said Sir Topham Hatt.

"I'll do it, Sir," said Toby quickly.

"Thank you," smiled Sir Topham Hatt. And before he could say anything else, Toby steamed off. He didn't want Sir Topham Hatt to tell him he was going to be put in a museum.

Toby waited impatiently at the flour mill. "Hurry up, hurry up," he *wheesh*ed. "I must get to the Docks as soon as I can."

When Toby delivered the flour, he saw Sir Topham Hatt standing on the dockside. He was talking to the Dock Master.

Sir Topham Hatt saw Toby. He wanted to speak to him, but Toby steamed off as fast as he could.

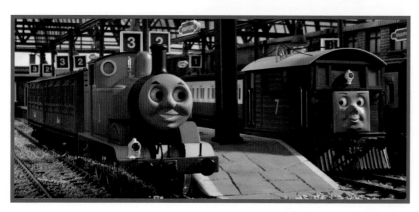

Later, Toby saw Thomas again. He was pulling Annie and Clarabel. "I'm off for my repaint," chuffed Thomas happily.

"I can pull Annie and Clarabel for you," said Toby.

"Thank you, Toby," tooted Thomas.

So Toby pulled Annie and Clarabel on Thomas' Branch Line.

And while James was getting a shiny new coat of red paint, Toby collected coal cars from the mine for James.

And while Percy was having *his* repaint, Toby shunted freight cars full of stone in the Quarry for Percy, even though it was dusty, dirty work.

At last, Toby had finished. He was very tired and very dirty.

Suddenly he saw Sir Topham Hatt waiting by the track. Toby still didn't want to speak to Sir Topham Hatt. Quickly he reversed into a siding and didn't see that a big rock had fallen on the line.

"Bust my cowcatchers!" he cried.

Luckily, no one was hurt. But Toby's axle and his cowcatchers were broken. He couldn't move!

Sir Topham Hatt hurried over. "Why have you been running away from me all day?" he asked.

"I—I don't want to be put in a museum," Toby said sadly.

"Why would I do *that*, Toby?" asked Sir Topham Hatt.

"Because a museum is full of old things and I'm an old steam tram. And I'm not Really Useful anymore."

Sir Topham Hatt smiled. "Toby, you may be old, but you are far too useful to be put in the museum. You have worked harder today than any other engine. And as Sodor's only steam tram, I have a very special job for you. First you will have a special polish. Then you are to take all the visitors to the museum for the Grand Opening."

Toby felt very happy. He let out a great *wheesh* of steam!

"I've been trying to tell you that all day," added Sir Topham Hatt.

Toby smiled. He felt very silly.

So Toby's axle and cowcatchers were repaired, and then he was polished until he looked as good as new.

On the day of the museum opening, Toby picked up the visitors at the Docks and puffed them proudly to the new museum.

Toby was proud to be old. And he was even prouder to be the only Really Useful Steam Tram on the Island of Sodor!

•Thomas and the New Engine•

The trains on the Island of Sodor keep very busy. There are always lots of jobs to do.

One morning, Sir Topham Hatt came to Tidmouth Sheds. "A new engine has arrived on the Island," he announced. "His name is Neville. You must all make him feel welcome. A happy engine is a Useful Engine."

Later, Thomas was stopped at a signal. The Signalman called down to Thomas. "The bridge ahead is unsafe. Thomas, you are to collect a piece of ironwork so the bridge can be repaired."

"Yes, sir," huffed Thomas.

At the yards, 'Arry and Bert were with Neville, the new engine. Neville was a steamie, but he had a square body like a diesel. Neville was backing up towards some trucks.

"Nearly there," said 'Arry cheekily.

"Nearly there," said Bert naughtily.

Then there was trouble!

"Watch where you're going, clumsy wheels!" 'Arry and Bert laughed.

Neville looked sad.

"It's not our fault if you're a silly steamie!" oiled Bert. And they laughed even harder.

Thomas arrived at the yards. He could see 'Arry and Bert laughing with Neville. "That must be the new engine," he thought. "He must be friends with the diesels."

Thomas arrived at Knapford Station.

"Have you seen the new engine yet?" asked James.

"Yes," said Thomas. "But we'd better be careful. I saw him at the yards with 'Arry and Bert. They were laughing together."

James was shocked! A steamie friendly with diesels?!?

As Thomas left, Edward pulled in.

"Have you heard about the new engine?" snorted James . . . and he started to tell Edward all about Neville.

Later, Edward was taking on water. He was talking to Percy. "That new steamie, Neville, is best friends with the diesels," Edward puffed. "He doesn't want to be with steamies at all."

"How do you know?" peeped Percy.

"James told me, and Thomas told him!" whistled Edward.

Later, Percy met Emily at a red signal.

"Don't go near Neville, the new engine," he told her. "The diesels have told him to biff into steamies. Edward told me—James told Edward—and they heard all about it from Thomas!"

When Thomas arrived at Abbey Station, Sir Topham Hatt was there. "Thomas, you must warn all engines not to cross the bridge until it's repaired," he boomed.

Thomas felt proud. It was a *very* useful job. Just then, he heard a whistle. Someone was coming! Thomas had to warn them. It was Neville . . . pulling *Annie and Clarabel*! Thomas was shocked! Annie and Clarabel were *his* carriages!

"Hello!" puffed Neville cheerfully.

"I'm not talking to you!" Thomas huffed crossly.

Neville didn't know what he had done.

Then Emily pulled in next to Neville. "Hello," said Neville happily.

Emily let out a *wheesh* of steam. "It's no use trying to make friends with me. I know you're going to biff into all the steamies! Just like 'Arry and Bert told you to!"

Thomas was surprised. But the Station Master blew his whistle. And Neville puffed sadly away.

"Where did you hear that Neville is going to biff into all the steamies?" Thomas asked Emily.

"Don't you know?" Emily whistled. "Percy told me, Edward told Percy, James told Edward, and *you* told James!" huffed Emily.

"But I only said to James that I'd seen Neville with 'Arry and Bert. . . ."

Then Toby arrived. "Have you heard about Neville, the new engine?" he puffed. "Henry saw 'Arry and Bert be horrible to him at the yards!"

Emily was shocked. Thomas couldn't believe it! Neville wasn't friends with the diesels after all!

"Where was Neville going?" Emily tooted.

"Cinders and ashes!" cried Thomas. "Neville's heading for the broken bridge! I must stop him!"

Neville was speeding through the countryside as fast as he could.

Suddenly Neville saw a barrier on the track. He slammed on his brakes, but it was too late. . . .

Neville was in terrible trouble! He was on the broken end of the bridge!

Thomas knew it was all his fault! Suddenly he had an idea! Thomas steamed slowly and carefully onto the bridge. He gently bumped Clarabel and was coupled up. Thomas was very scared. Slowly and steadily, he began to pull Neville back from the edge. The bridge made a creaking noise. Thomas knew he must hurry! He pulled as hard as he could. . . .

And with one big puff, he pulled Neville's wheels off the bridge! Thomas had done it! He had saved Neville and Annie and Clarabel!

"Thank you," whistled Neville.

"I should have warned you," puffed Thomas. "But I was too busy believing silly stories. I thought you didn't like steamies. But now I know I was wrong."

Thomas gave Neville a long, friendly *toot toot*.

Neville was very happy. At last, he knew he had a good friend in Thomas.